S0-AHO-824

al-Saʿif fī al-ṣukhrah
Maccarone, Grace.
JUV/E/ AL PB 10 141 .M32 DISCARD

السيف في الصخرة

No part of this publication may be reproduced in whole or in part, or stored in a retrieval system, or transmitted in any form or by any means, electronic, mechanical, photocopying, recording, or otherwise, without written permission of the publisher. For information regarding permission write to Scholastic Inc., 557 Broadway, New York, NY 10012.

Text copyright © 1992 by Grace Maccarone.
Illustrations copyright © 2003 by Joseph Boddy.
Activities copyright © 2003 Scholastic Inc.
First printing, September 1992.
All rights reserved. Published by Scholastic Inc.
SCHOLASTIC and associated logos are trademarks and/or registered trademarks of Scholastic Inc.

ISBN 978-0-439-86399-5

First Arabic Edition, 2006. Printed in China.

1 2 3 4 5 6 7 8 9 10 62 11 10 09 08 07

ލިޔެގެންދިނީ: މާގްރީ ޑިޕައޮލާ • ތަރުޖަމާ: ޢަބްދުﷲ ޞާދިޤް

ފާދިރީ މޮގުރީ އާއި
ޖާދޫގަރު

R0353P PP759

ᠲᠡᠷᠡ ᠨᠢ ᠨᠠᠳᠠᠳᠤ ᠮᠠᠰᠢ ᠰᠠᠶᠢᠬᠠᠨ ᠰᠠᠨᠠᠭᠳᠠᠭᠰᠠᠨ ᠶᠤᠮ᠃

قالَ الرَّجُلُ الطَّويلُ السَّمينُ:
«سَوْفَ أَكونُ الْمَلِكَ».
قالَ الرَّجُلُ الْقَصيرُ النَّحيفُ:
«سَوْفَ أَكونُ الْمَلِكَ».

قالَ الرَّجُلُ الطَّويلُ النَّحيفُ: «سَوْفَ أَكونُ الْمَلِكَ».

قالَ النّاسُ:
«يَجِبُ أَنْ تَنْتَهِيَ الْحَرْبُ!»
وَذَهَبوا إِلى مَنْزِلِ الَّذي يَعْرِفُ
الْكَثيرَ مِنَ الأُمورِ.
وَقالَ بَعْضُهُمْ إِنَّهُ رَجُلٌ حَكيمٌ.
قالَ النّاسُ: «نُريدُ مَلِكًا».

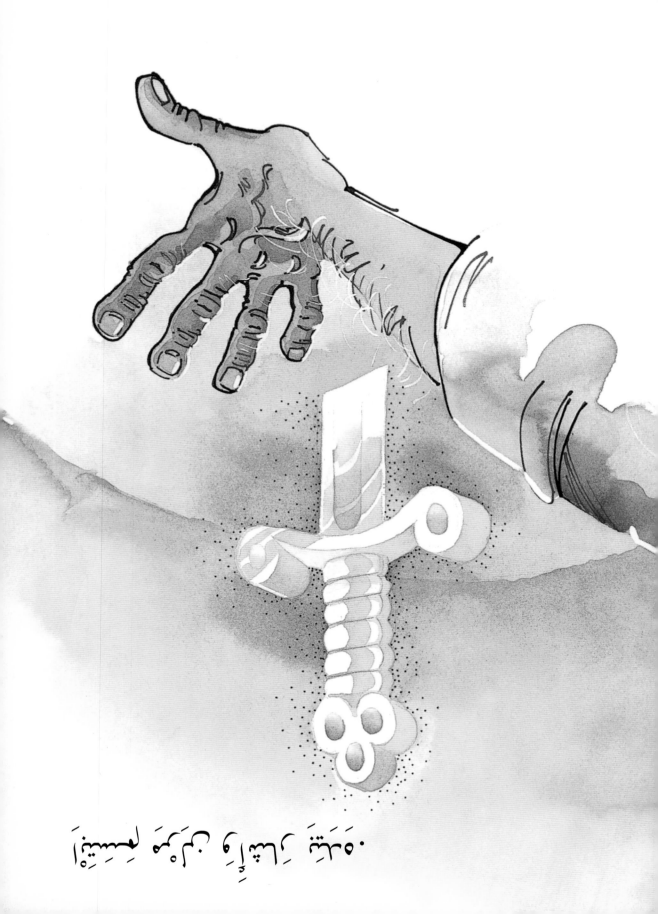

ތުނޑުކޮޅެއްގެ މަތީގައި ކަނޑި ނަގައިފި.

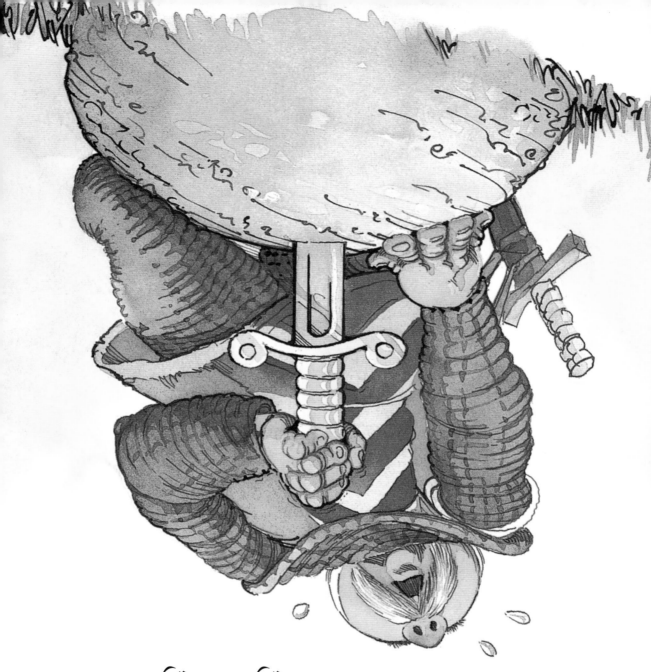

ᕮᑊᒣᕈ, ᕮᑊᒣᕈ.

ᕌᔭᕈ ᕮᑊᒣᕈ, ᕮᑊᒣᕈ, ᕌᔭᕈ.

"ᕌᔭᑊᒣᕈ ᕈᔭ!"

ᕌᔭᑊᒣᕈᑊᒣᕈ ᕈᔭ ᕮᑊᒣᕈ ᕈᔭ ᕌᔭᕈ:

ᡝᠵᡝᠨ᠂ ᡝᠵᡝᠨ᠂

ᡠᠯᡳ᠌ ᡝᠵᡝᠨ᠂ ᡝᠵᡝᠨ᠂

"ᠨᡳᠶᠠᠯᠮᠠ!"

ᠠᠨ ᡳᠯᠠ ᡳᠨᡝᠩᡤᡳ ᡝᡵᡤᡝᠯᡝᠮᡝ ᠪᡳᡥᡝ᠄

ᡝᡥᡝ ᠪᡳᡵᡝᡳ ᠠᠯᡳ ᡳᠵᡠᠯᡝᠮᡝ ᡳᠯᠠ ᡝᡳᠮᠠᠯᠠᠮᡝ᠄

ᠪᡳ ᠠᡳ ᠯᠠ ᡳᠯᠠ ᡳᠯᠠ ᡝᡵᡤᡝᠯᡝᠮᡝ ᠪᡳᠮᡝ᠄

لكِنَّ الرَّجُلَ القَصيرَ النَّحيفَ لَمْ يَسْتَطِعْ أَنْ يَسْحَبَ السَّيْفَ مِنَ الصَّخْرَةِ.

قالَ الرَّجُلُ الطَّويلُ النَّحيفُ: «أَنا أَسْتَطيعُ! أَنا أَسْتَطيعُ!»

وَقالَ الرَّجُلُ القَصيرُ السَّمينُ: «أَنا أَسْتَطيعُ! أَنا أَسْتَطيعُ!»

لِكِنَّهُما لَمْ يَسْتَطيعا أَنْ
يَسْحَبا السَّيْفَ مِنَ الصَّخْرَةِ.
حاوَلَ أَفْرادُ الشَّعْبِ كُلُّهُمْ،
وَ لَمْ يَسْتَطِعْ أَحَدٌ أَنْ يَنْجَحَ،
فَيَسْحَبَ السَّيْفَ مِنَ الصَّخْرَةِ.
وَهكَذا، اِسْتَمَرَّتِ الْحَرْبُ.

اِسْتَمَرَّ الرِّجالُ الْكِبارُ في الْقِتالِ.

وَاسْتَمَرَّ الشَّبابُ في الْقِتالِ.

وَاسْتَمَرَّ الصِّغارُ يَخْتَبِئونَ
بَيْنَ الشُّجَيْراتِ، وَيُراقِبونَ.

وَكانَ آرْثِر لا يَزالُ بَيْنَهُمْ.

ܒܝܝܟ ܫܘܬܝܬ ܘܓ ܗܟܘܢ ܒܢ ܐܝܫ

ܐܡܪ ܐܟ ܡܠܐ

ܚܒ ܒܝܝܟ ܓ ܡܢ ܒ ܗ ܠܐܚܘ

ܐܚܝ ܒ ܚܝ

ܫܘ ܟ ܟ ܐ ܒܝܬ ܐܢ

ޖައްސަވައި ގެންދިޔަ ޚަބަރު.
ރ ޖެއްސެވި ގޮތުގައި ޚަބަރު.
ރ ޖެއްސަވައި ގެންދިޔަ ޚަބަރު.
ރ ޖައްސަވައި ގޮތުގައި ޚަބަރު.

ޕުއްޕެ ގައި ދޫ
ޕުއްޕެ ގައި ސާފު.
ޕުއްޕެ ގޮއި.

ﮐﯘﺳﺘﺴﻦ ﺋﯘ ﺋﯧﮕﯩﺰﻻﺷﺘﯘﺭﯗﭖ ﺋﺎﯕﻼ

ﺋﯧﯖﯩﺰ ﺋﯘ ﺷﯘﮬﯘﺭ ﺗﯘﺭ ﺗﺎﻏﺪﺍ

ﺷﯘﯕﺎ ﺋﺎﻧﺎ ﮬﯧﻠﯩﻘﻰ ﺋﯘ ﺗﺎﻏﺪﺍ

ﺧﯘﺷﭙﯘﺭﺍﻕ ﺑﯘﻟﯘﭖ ﯞﺍﺳﯩﺮﺍ

ﻣﯘﻣﺎ ﮬﯧﻠﯩﻘﻰ ﺋﯘ ﺗﺎﻏﺪﺍ

ܘܐܣܬܟܠ ܕܚܕ ܗܘ ܘܠܐ ܝܬܝܪ

ܘܐܬܒܣܡ ܠܦܘܬ ܡܐܝܟ ܗܘ

ܠܒܓܢܝܐ ܒܡܪܚܘܩ ܟܢܝܫܐܝ

ܗܪܟܐ ܚܙܐ ܐܢܐ ܝܬ ܝܬܝܐ ܬܡܢ

To Three Special Sisters—
Rose, Kay, and Fran
        —*Harriet Lerner and Susan Goldhor*

To Rachel and Lily—
        —*Catharine O'Neill*

What's So Terrible About Swallowing an Apple Seed?

By Harriet Lerner and Susan Goldhor

Illustrated by Catharine O'Neill

HARPERCOLLINS*PUBLISHERS*

One day, Rosie and her big sister, Katie, were sitting in their favorite tree eating crisp red apples.

"Crunch, crunch, crunch," crunched Rosie.

"Munch, munch, munch," munched Katie.

Crunching and munching and munching and crunching, Rosie and Katie ate their apples right down to the core.

Suddenly Rosie said, "I swallowed an apple seed! Whoops! I swallowed another one," and she giggled.

"Oh, no," said Katie in her most worried voice. "Watch out!"

"Why?" asked Rosie. "What's so terrible about swallowing an apple seed?"

Katie thought fast. "Well," she said, trying to sound smart, "that apple seed is going to grow into a tree right inside your stomach. That's what's so terrible."

"But how can it grow into a tree inside my stomach?" asked Rosie.

"It's easy," answered Katie. "It's nice and warm down there. It's just the right place for a seed to grow."

Rosie thought for a long time. "But trees need sunshine to grow. It's dark in my stomach."

"Well, of course," said Katie. Like most big sisters, she always had an answer for everything. "It's dark in the ground, too, when you plant seeds there. But when the branches of your apple tree get big enough, they'll grow out of your ears and get all the sunshine they need."

Rosie sat very still. She thought she could feel the tree starting to grow inside her stomach.

"What should I do, Katie?" she asked.

"Let's keep it secret till the branches start to show," said Katie.

"Okay," said Rosie. She always thought that her big sister knew best.

Every night Rosie asked Katie to look in her ears with a flashlight to see how the apple tree was growing.

Every night Katie said, "I can see it! I can see it! I'm almost sure I can see the tip of a branch down there!"

And every night Rosie could not fall asleep for a long time. She could feel her ears itching, and she tried to imagine what she would look like with apple tree branches growing out of her ears. Rosie imagined a lot of problems.

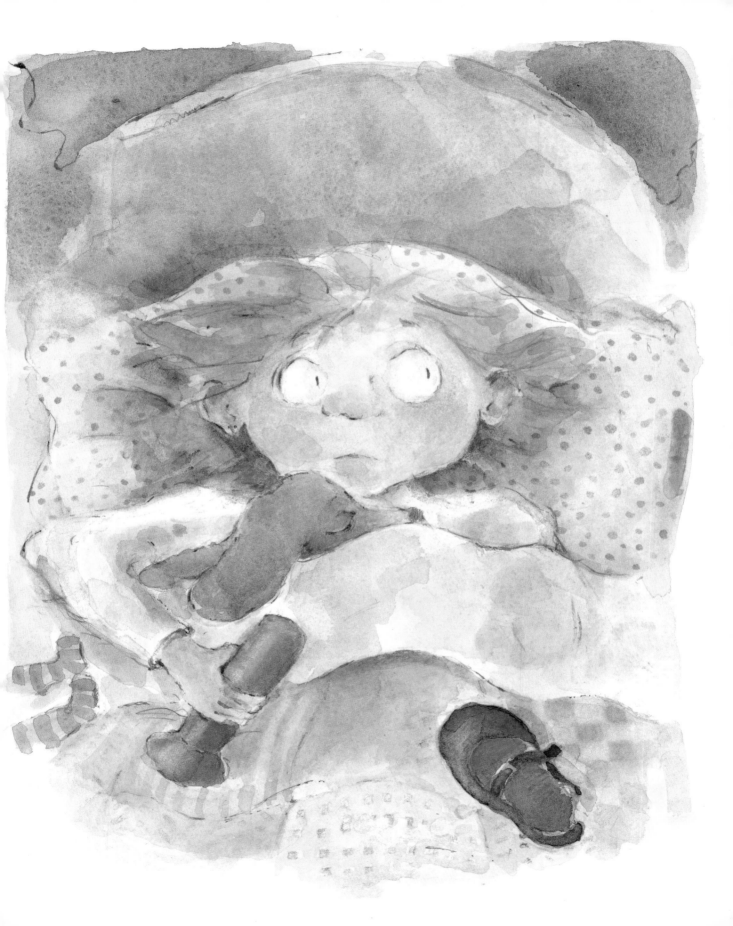

None of her hats would fit.

She wouldn't fit through the school-bus door.

No more somersaults and handstands!

Or jump rope!

Good-bye, haircuts!
She would have to go
to the woodcutter instead.

All she could be when she grew up

was a coat rack.

Rosie felt very sad.

Pretty soon Katie began to feel sad, too.

She knew a seed couldn't really grow in Rosie's

stomach. And she hadn't known that a lie could grow

so big, just like a seed grows into a tree. The bigger

the lie got, the harder it was for Katie to tell Rosie

the truth. So she used her imagination to cheer Rosie

up. Every night she would sit on Rosie's bed and tell

her all the good things about having branches grow-

ing out of her ears.

Rosie could reach up and pick an apple
any time she wanted.

When they went to the beach, they would always have a shady spot to sit.

If Rosie got lost at the ball game,

they would always be able to find her.

Rosie would never get lost again.

All their friends could climb up
and play on the branches.

On birthdays they could decorate her
branches with ribbons and candles.

All the animals would be her friends.

Rosie felt much better. She told her friend Bonnie that she had a special secret.

"Tell me! Tell me!" begged Bonnie. "I'm your best friend."

Rosie handed Bonnie the flashlight. "Look in my ears," she said.

"I don't see anything," Bonnie said. "Just a little ear dirt."

"Don't you see a branch?" asked Rosie.

"Nope," said Bonnie.

Rosie thought about this for a long time. She got madder and madder. Then she went and found Katie.

"Bonnie looked in my ear," she told her big sister, "and she didn't see any tree! You told me a lie!"

Katie said, "I can't help it if you believe everything I say!" But inside she was glad that the lie was finally over. She hugged Rosie and said she was sorry.

"It's okay," Rosie said. "But I was starting to like my apple tree."

The itch in Rosie's ears went away, and that night when she got into bed she thought how nice it was to be like everybody else. But as she was falling asleep, she started to feel a little bit sad.

"Katie," Rosie said, "I miss my apple tree!"

Katie understood. So she told Rosie a wonderful story about a little girl with apple tree branches growing out of her ears. In the spring, the little girl's head would be covered with apple blossoms. In the summer, birds would build nests and squirrels would play in her branches. In the fall, she would bring apples to school for everyone to eat.

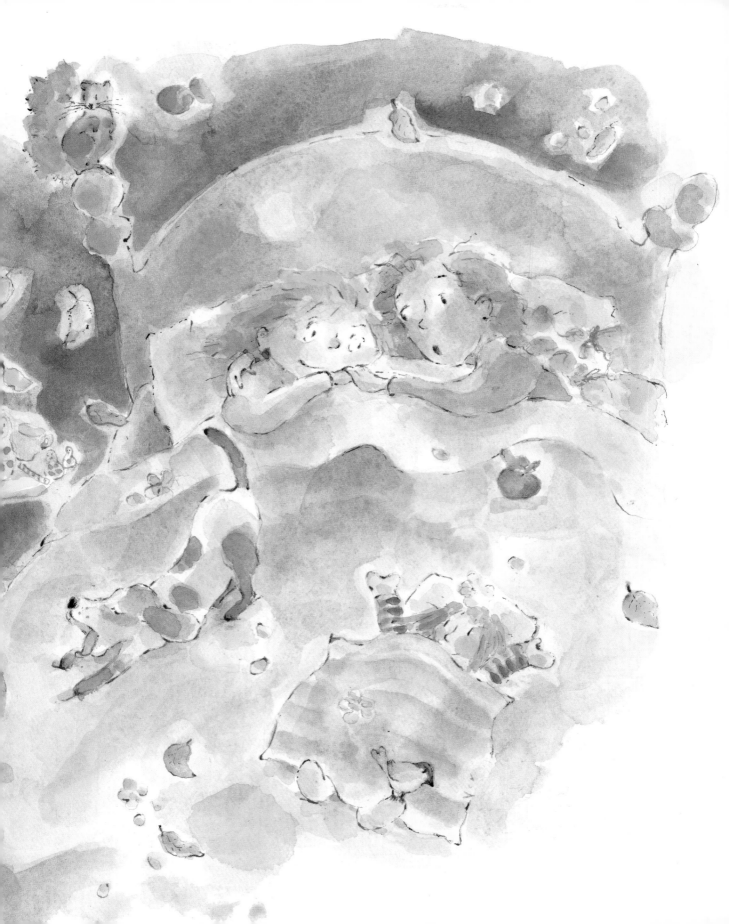

And before Katie even got to winter,

Rosie was fast asleep.

What's So Terrible About Swallowing an Apple Seed?
Text copyright © 1996 by Harriet Lerner and Susan
Goldhor Illustrations copyright © 1996 by Catharine O'Neill
Printed in the U.S.A. All rights reserved.
Library of Congress
Cataloging-in-Publication Data Lerner, Harriet. What's so
terrible about swallowing an apple seed? / by Harriet Lerner and
Susan Goldhor ; illustrated by Catharine O'Neill.   p.   cm.
Summary: When Rosie swallows an apple seed, her sister
Katie tells her that an apple tree will grow out of her ears.
ISBN 0-06-024523-9. — ISBN 0-06-024524-7 (lib. bdg.)
[1. Sisters—Fiction.   2. Honesty—Fiction.]   I. Goldhor, Susan.
II. O'Neill,   Catharine, ill.   III. Title. PZ7.L5595Wh 1996
94-2769 [E]—dc20   CIP   AC   Typography by Al Cetta
1 2 3 4 5 6 7 8 9 10   ❖   First Edition